Journey to the Surface of the Earth.

By John McCarron

Illustrator Frank Muldowney

First published in 2025 by Blossom Spring Publishing
Journey To The Surface Of The Earth
Copyright © 2025 John McCarron.
ISBN 978-1-0683266-6-0
E: admin@blossomspringpublishing.com
W: www.blossomspringpublishing.com

Chapter 1
The Three Bears

Jimmy and John — born on the same day 17 years and 364 days ago — lifelong friends, will die tomorrow. Destiny has determined death at 18 years of age. Glorious selflessness for the greater good of all brothers and sisters. But they didn't want glory. They liked life. An escape plan had been hatched. Which way to go?

"I think left," John said.

"Left. Right?" Jimmy said.

"No just left," John said.

"Yes, left. Right?" Jimmy said.

"No right, just left," John said.

"I know, that's what I said, left, that's right."

"Oh right, right."

"Let's sleep on it, right?"

"Ok, goodnight."

In the morning before anyone else was around, they slipped away. Leftwards. It was their glorious destiny.

The Earth, Mother Earth, steamrolled to Extinction, humanity at the helm. A subterranean world had been created and the chosen few, admitted. The others who were left behind could take their chances elsewhere.

Jimmy and John are a generational subsequent of the chosen few and as such they are to abide by the rules and laws.

"Are you sure this is the right way?" Jimmy stated.

"Put it down to instinct," John said, "and if we're wrong, we can always go back, a'dare say,"

"Well anyway, how do we know if we're going in the wrong direction?" Jimmy said.

"That's a very good point, maybe left and right are both ok, a'dare say," said John.

"Is that instinct again do you think?" said Jimmy.

They were on their way. The boys were uncertain. They can't think what's ahead but know what's behind. Their forefathers, realising living space in their new, clean, healthy and self-replenishing environment was limited, decided a cull at 18 years of age was necessary. Mental and physical wellbeing decline from that point and so it's time to go heroically. Mortal fear doesn't exist. They were to be whisked away in a vehicle, 'the Capsule of Spiritual Yearning', (C.O.S.Y.) to their ultimate glorious destination. The boys stumbled along their way for a long time.

"A'dare say," John said again.

"Who's A. D'Arcy?" said Jimmy.

"No, it's not, A. D'Arcy, it's a'dare say," said John.

"Well what does it mean, a'dare say? It's a new one for you," said Jimmy.

John thought for a moment. He wasn't even aware that he had said anything unusual. "Well, a'dare say, is only a figure of speech. 'A' refers to me, as in 'I'. 'Dare say' means, I'm not 100% sure of what I'm saying, or of what I've just heard, but in all likelihood, I believe it to be correct and therefore I'm prepared to agree if I have just heard it, or I'm emphasising I believe it to be true if I've just said it."

Jimmy's eyes had glazed over and he hoped they were going in the right direction. He promised himself to ask no more questions.

Mother Earth and all she meant, blemished, tarnished and poisoned by the very children she had nourished and nurtured. There they were, even now, deep within her bowels suckling her marrow once more.

As they walked, they saw, heard and smelt all the things along the route, a straight left line with no apparent end.

"It's been a long day, I'm hungry and tired," Jimmy finally said.

"A'dare say," said John.

"Well, are you not hungry at least?" asked Jimmy.

"I am. I could eat the leg of a grand piano, per sé," said John.

"Well, what do you mean, you could eat the leg of a grand piano Percy?" inquired Jimmy.

"No, not the leg of a grand piano Percy, but the leg of a grand piano per sé," said John.

"Well, what do you mean?" said Jimmy.

"It's just a figure of speech and what I mean is…if all there was to eat was the leg of a grand piano, I could eat it, that's how hungry I am. Look, it's unlikely that we are going to come across the leg of a grand piano on this road, but if I did, I could eat it. I'm not saying I would eat it, but that's just how hungry I am. It's the 'hungry' bit that's the important part. That's per sé."

Jimmy knew he could eat the leg of a chair and was very confused, he was about to say something when a small, old cottage appeared in front of them; they were suddenly in the middle of a forest, with very tall conifer trees. They were surrounded by the aroma of beautiful, enchanting, enhancing refreshment. They gingerly approached the door of the cottage and peered through its window. There didn't appear to be any sign of life.

They split up. Jimmy went to the right and John to the left, but nothing stirred. At the back of the cottage, they found a window looking out onto a small garden and into a kitchen. On the kitchen table were three steaming bowls of porridge: one large, one medium-sized and one small. All their fears disappeared, and they rushed to the kitchen door and sprang through it. John picked up a big spoon and ladled the porridge from the big bowl into his mouth.

"Whoa!" he yelped, spat out the porridge and breathed heavily in and out to cool his burnt mouth. "That's scalding. I'll try the medium-sized one. Whoa! Still too hot! I'll try the small one. Ahh, that's just fine for me. I'll have this one. You can have the middle one but take it easy, don't burn yourself," John said.

4

"For someone who could eat the leg of a grand piano not so long ago, you're very fussy," Jimmy replied.

They ate all the porridge, after a bit of time to let it cool down.

Jimmy yawned, "I could do with a sleep. I'll take a look around and see if there's a place to lie down."

Sure enough, there was a big bed in the bedroom. It was a bit hard, but he got in anyway and fell fast asleep immediately. John got in beside him and also slept straight away.

They were awoken by a terrifying, angry, growling roar coming from the kitchen.

"Who's been eating my porridge? If I find out, woe betide," said a booming voice.

"Don't worry," said a more sedate, calming voice, "I can make some more. You go and mind Junior, sit down and read your paper."

Jimmy and John were lying trembling in the bed, fearing the worst. After a while, they heard footsteps approaching the bedroom door.

John said, "We'd better get out and get in under the bed."

Jimmy replied, "What do you mean we'd better get out and get 'in' under the bed? How can you get 'in' the bed and get under the bed at the same time? Is that another of your figures of speech?"

John said, "You'd better get under the bed A'Darcy."

A foul-smelling, fearsome-looking bear entered the

room. He was clearly not in the best of form by the tone of his seething low growls.

Who's been sleeping in my bed? He thought, but still, he slumped to the bed. His wife followed shortly and lay down gently next to him.

"I can't tolerate this breach of our home Mama. We can't appear to be an easy target for every Tom, Dick, Harry and John," growled the big angry bear.

John squirmed under the bed.

"Tomorrow I will go out, and seek out, and find the perpetrators. I will tear their hearts from their chests, and their intestines from their abdomens and spread all their bits around our home as a warning to anyone who thinks they can come in here and take our porridge."

Jimmy gulped quietly.

"Did you hear that?" said the big bear.

"Now don't get all worked up, it was nothing, Papa. Try and get some sleep and we'll talk about it tomorrow. After all, it was only a bit of porridge and we don't want to worry Junior," said Mama Bear.

"Hmph grr," said Papa Bear and fell fast asleep with a roaring snore.

Mama Bear settled into a slumber and started snoring in tandem with Papa Bear.

John nudged Jimmy, indicating for him to get out from 'in' under the bed. Jimmy nudged John a bit more abruptly indicating that he should go first.

John said quietly, "You go first you'd be better at it

than me,"

Jimmy replied more loudly, "No I wouldn't, I was never 'in' under a bed in my life, so I can't see how I could be better than you at getting out from 'in' under the bed! You go first you're nearer the door,"

With that, Junior popped in through the door and spied the two boys 'in' under the bed and let out a big scream, "Papa, Papa, they're in under the bed!"

There was no hesitation from the boys now and they both sprang out from 'in under the bed', shot past Junior, out the bedroom door and out the front door. Jimmy took the time to remark to Junior as he bolted past him, "You can't be in the bed and under the bed at the same time. Come on!"

They turned left and ran straight as fast as their legs could carry them, leaving in their wake, the loudest growling roar from Papa Bear that woke the whole forest from its slumber.

They ran and ran until they could run no more. They blew and wheezed and spluttered and fell down in a heap clutching their sides. They hoped they were safe but could do no more about it; they were in a state of utter exhaustion.

After a while of recovering and no further noise from that great big Papa bear, John said to Jimmy, "Well that was a lucky escape. Why did you have to make all that fuss and commotion in under the bed, you woke Junior Bear up, you blithering idiot."

Jimmy replied, "Who do you think you are calling a blithering idiot? You started it poking and nudging me to get out from in under the bed. You should have got out first if you thought the coast was clear and I'd have followed."

John said, "Well you're a lot more athletic than me and more nimble. I just thought you'd be better at it than me." Jimmy replied, "As I've said already, I was never 'in' under a bed ever in my life! So how could I be better at it than you? Can you answer me that one?"

John said, "A'dare say I can't answer that one, and a'dare say we should be getting on our way before some other big Papa takes offence at us."

How was it that such a situation as Jimmy and John found themselves, arose in the first place? Ok, so they have left their subterranean home but where did it really come from? What provoked its necessity? It was rumoured that when man inhabited the Earth's crust, amongst other fiendish, deadly weaponry, there existed instruments to achieve total annihilation of a life-supporting environment. Several parties had access to these devices and a mutual accord existed whereby, no one party would let off one of their devices because the response would be the end of everything, (mutually assured destruction, M.A.D).

A status quo existed for many years. The instruments of doom lay idly by and gathering dust. One day, one of them was triggered and sent into orbit. Some people say it was accidental; a person of an unknown denomination had come upon a big red push button in a long-neglected office of a government building and said, "I wonder what this button is for?"

Others say a deranged megalomaniacal zealot had access to the button. Either way, with that first trajectory, other retaliatory missiles followed and achieved total annihilation on the Earth's crust, but under the Earth's crust, the chosen few had scarpered once the fireworks had started, to their new home which had been created for them.

Chapter 2
Mirror, Mirror, on the Wall

Well enough of that, let's see what the lads were getting up to. They had dusted themselves down as best they could after their adventures, and gone about their way, left and straight.

"You look a bit of a shambles," John said to Jimmy.

"What do you mean I look a bit of a shambles? You should take a look at yourself! You are a total shambles," said Jimmy.

"Take a look at myself? You are the most shambolic individual I have ever seen. You're dirty, your hair is all matted and you smell," replied John.

Jimmy said, "If you could see yourself now, *and* smell yourself by the way, you'd run and hide yourself away! I wish we had a mirror so you could see what I see."

"Yeah, I wish we had a mirror and then you'd be quiet for once."

With that, the boys found themselves in a big, spooky old castle in front of a very tall mirror attached to the wall in a grand, high-vaulted, ancient and cobwebbed hall.

"Whoa!!" said John, "Who do those two tramps think they are looking at?"

Footsteps approached the hall and John said, "Let's push this cabinet here out from the wall and get in behind it so no one sees us."

"What do you mean 'get in behind it'? How can you get 'in' it and behind it at the same time?" said Jimmy.

The hall door began to creak open.

"For heaven's sake just pull it out a little and we'll hide ourselves," said John.

So, they eased it away from the wall and made sure that they couldn't be seen 'in' behind it. They couldn't see out from it and were well hidden.

The hall door opened fully, and a young man stepped into the hall. He was dressed in a starched and ironed white shirt and black trousers. He stood perfectly straight at the opened door and into the room entered a most serene female figure. She wore a golden crown studded with jewels upon her beautifully coiffed hair. She was adorned with large, pearl teardrop earrings, a shimmering and dazzling necklace, bracelets of gold and rings of emerald and sapphires. Her dress was of black satin upon which flowered white and yellow narcissi. Her legs were hidden by the train of her gown, but the boys just about got a peek and they could well imagine. They let slip a timid gasp and gulp.

The serene lady, stood in front of the mirror and said, "Mirror, Mirror, on the wall, who is the fairest of them all?"

The mirror replied, "Thou art my Queen, thou art the
fairest of them all."

She was about to move away, when the mirror

continued, "As for those two tramps in behind that cabinet over there beside the wall, please do not allow them to present themselves in front of me ever again! Otherwise, I will shatter myself as an act of terminal disgust."

The Queen turned and paced royally over towards the cabinet.

"Come out from in behind that cabinet," she commanded.

John nudged Jimmy to go out first. Jimmy nudged John more brusquely for him to go first. John whispered, "You go first you'd be better at it than me."

Jimmy was about to say that he didn't know how John could work that one out, as he'd never hidden 'in' behind a cabinet before, when two burly men pulled the cabinet away from the wall exposing the two squabbling and then sheepish boys.

"Bring them to the dungeons whilst I decide what to do with them," ordered the Queen.

So the two boys were brought out of the hall, through a long corridor, down some steps, into the dungeons where they were escorted into a single cell with a single bed and single bucket in it. The door slammed shut and a clanking key turned the lockbolt across. They were imprisoned.

"I wonder what the bucket is for?" said Jimmy.

"We'll find out a' dare say," said John.

The Queen ruled her queendom with a rod of iron (or

anything else that came to hand). She had recently poisoned that poor girl Snow White who had been masquerading around the place as the fairest one of them all. She was in reality a wicked witch. Her dominance was supreme and nobody dared doubt her wonderfulness and munificence. But she was bored, and the appearance of the two tramps had intrigued her. She decided that it would be great sport to see what was beneath the trampish appearances of the two men hiding 'in' behind her cabinet and now festering down in the dungeons. So, she ordered her butlers to bring them hence to have them bathed and scrubbed, coiffed, manicured and pedicured and redressed in the outfits of the princes she had once dated and married over the years but who had become tiresome and irksome and whom she had discarded discreetly.

Meanwhile, Jimmy and John were wondering how on earth they were discovered 'in' behind the cabinet up against the wall.

John said, "You nudged me too firmly and it upset an ornament on top of the cabinet."

Jimmy replied, "You didn't hide yourself well enough and the mirror could see your legs beneath the cabinet. There's no way mine could be seen because I was directly behind the leg of the cabinet and what's more, my trousers are the same colour as the colour of the wall, so they blended in perfectly."

John looked a bit forlorn, and Jimmy said, "I suppose

the mirror could have seen us going in behind the cabinet in the first place. We weren't to know that the mirror would talk."

Just then the clank of a key unlocked the cell door and they were ushered out and up to the bathing rooms to be washed and scrubbed and generally cleaned up and reclothed. They were shaved, washed, conditioned and pomaded. Their fingernails were filed and polished and their toenails received similar treatment. Their cheeks were rouged and their brows plucked and shaped. Rings were placed upon their fingers and fine linen shirts upon their backs. Velvet suits were sized for them and placed on their shoulders and legs. Silver buckled shoes were horned onto their feet. A fine mist of perfume was puffed about their beings. They were beautified beyond recognition and even looked upon each other with utmost admiration.

They were escorted once more to the great hall and past the tall mirror hanging on the wall. As they passed by, they stuck their tongues out at it, for giving them away earlier that day.

Jimmy said to the mirror, "Reflect on this, you can't be 'in' the cabinet and 'behind' the cabinet at the same time, duh!" John told him to get a move on as they had a very important date.

They were brought over to the Queen who was at the far end of the hall sitting by a large open fire, admiring her fingernails. She looked up and smiled. A favourable visage came upon her countenance on seeing the two former trampish men. She approvingly assented for them to come and sit beside her.

"Now, how I see what a change has come over you both," she said, "you are no longer dirty and smelly and rough, but are really quite attractive. We will dine at nine. I must take my leave now and retire to my boudoir. I have important business to attend to. So until nine, you may amuse yourselves as you wish."

With that, she stood and walked majestically to take her leave out of the hall. As she passed by the mirror, she admired her reflection and asked once more; "Mirror, mirror on the wall, who is the fairest of them all?"

The mirror replied tremulously, "Jimmy and John fair Queen. Jimmy and John art the fairest of them all."

If the boys thought Papa Bear had made a racket, it was nothing compared to the tumultuous outpouring of the Queen. She was louder than a volcanic explosion from Krakatoa in the Indonesian Ocean. The mirror shattered and fell to the floor in many shards, which for their impudence the Queen trampled and spat on each and every one until all that was left, was over ten million glistening grains of sand in a pool of Queen spit.

She called her henchmen to come and take Jimmy and John away and forthwith chop their heads off and disfigure their faces into an uglier sight, even more than a blobfish sitting at the bottom of the Tasmanian Sea.

John said to the Queen, "Shhh! Don't take it so

personally the mirror is just a bit mixed up, a' dare say."

"WHAAAT?" screamed the Queen, and John was about to begin to explain the derivation of, 'A'dare say', but Jimmy noticed her clenched white knuckles and smoke coming from her ears and nostrils, and for once asked no questions and made a break for the hall door. John followed in his footsteps. They scooted around the approaching henchmen down the corridor and out the front door. They just managed to crawl under the descending portcullis. They passed by bins from the castle piled high with rubbish from the Queen's court, on top of which they spotted their old clothes which they grabbed on their way. They turned left and ran in a straight line as fast as their legs could carry them until they could run no more and fell to the ground in a heap, totally exhausted.

Chapter 3
The Midas Touch

Jimmy and John were on their feet and ready to continue their journey, leftwards and straight. Firstly, they changed back into their old clothes, which were far more trendy. Their initial trudge turned into a jaunty stroll. They were glad to be alive, to see, hear and smell all the wonderful sights, sounds and aromas that surrounded them.

"Whatever happens down the road will surely not present such demons as we have already encountered," said John poetically. Jimmy wasn't paying attention but just soaking it all in. Back in the sanctum, anything you desired could be got. Here though, we're new things never before dreamed of. In the Sanctum desires were limited to what you could imagine. There was however no need for improvements as everything worked perfectly. There was no need for possessions as everyone owned everything.

"Well? What do you think? Do you think we will meet more and worse trouble along our way?" said John, slightly annoyed for being ignored.

"Oh! What? Yea...no. I don't know, and I don't care either. What difference does it make? Ok we've had a couple of close encounters, even brushes with death but we're faced with that wherever we go, home or here," Jimmy replied.

"Well, I suppose that's so, a' dare say. If all our encounters end up with us running for our lives, to get away and we're not doing anything wrong in the first place, then something's wrong. At home, we had nothing but needed for nothing. We knew no other way. Here we have nothing but need for something, anything. To possess something worthwhile and valuable," said John.

"What's more worthwhile and valuable if food, air and water are not? Then what is?" asked Jimmy.

"Well take for example the headpiece upon that demonic, not the fairest of them all, 'hic', I wouldn't mind having that," said John.

"What do you mean, 'hic'? You have the hiccups a' dare say. Now you've got me saying it. Hold your nose, put your fingers in your ears and drink some water all at the same time. That'll cure them hiccups, guaranteed!" replied Jimmy.

"How can you do all those things at the one time?" responded John.

Jimmy proceeded to give John a physical demonstration of the guaranteed cure of the hiccups by putting his little fingers in his ears, twisting the palms of his hands upright and placing his thumbs over his nostrils whilst bending down and tilting his head under an imaginary tap. Realising he hadn't turned on the imaginary tap, he straightened himself up, turned on the tap and then repeated the first part of the 'guaranteed cure of the hiccups'.

"You never mentioned the tap when you first told me of the guaranteed cure," said John. Jimmy got John to follow his instructions for the guaranteed cure, placing his thumbs over his nostrils, turning his palms upwards, and placing his little fingers in his ears. He got him to bend beneath an imaginary tap and pretended he was turning it on. Eventually, John got impatient with this tiresome masquerade and stood straight up with his hands by his side.

"Well?" said Jimmy.

"Well, what?" replied John.

"Well, how's the hiccups?" said Jimmy.

"I don't have the hiccups," replied John.

"Well, there you are then! I told you it was a guaranteed cure," said Jimmy.

"I never had the hiccups in the first place, what are you blathering on about," said John.

"Well, why did you say 'hic' then in that case?" asked Jimmy.

"I was quoting what the mirror mirror on the wall said," said John disdainfully.

"What?" said Jimmy.

"Yea, when you say 'hic', after something it means that the words you just said before you say 'hic' are exactly what was said, by the mirror, in this case," said John.

"That doesn't make much sense to me," Jimmy said. "Why do you have to go about everything in such a convoluted way? What's more, as far as I can remember the mirror mirror on the wall said firstly, "Thou art the fairest of them all, oh Fair Queen!" and then said secondly, "Jimmy art the fairest of them all," when it got a better look at me, sick. 'Sic' you mean sic, not hic, it's sic."

John was going to correct Jimmy's fanciful memory but then thought better of arguing with such a big nincompoop as this feeble-minded moron beside him. Instead, he said, "Well what do you think then?"

"What do I think of what?"

"What do you think of the Evil Queen's Crown? Whatever about her, and her vainglorious temper, what about her crown? It was made of the most beautiful materials I have ever seen, and why can't I have it or anything like it? Just to be in its presence was daunting, but to possess it? What must that be like? No wonder she had such a high opinion of herself with it sitting on top of her head," extolled John.

"Well, now that you say it, and it never did occur to me before, I think you are onto something now that you have pointed out its magnificence and deluxeness. I too desire to be in its presence, even to possess it." Jimmy conceded.

Jimmy and John found themselves within the walls of a great castle, in a beautiful rose garden. The weather was balmy and the fragrance from the roses was hypnotic. They spied the figure of a very important-looking man sweeping majestically and hysterically through the garden. They took up a vantage point behind a potting shed and viewed the scene in amazement. The important-looking man occasionally stretched down his hands touched a rose and shortly after, let out a voluble 'whoop!' They may as well have taken a closer look because the man was in a complete bubble of a frenzied and orgasmically entranced, rapturous tour of the garden. Occasionally the important-looking man bent down as if to smell the roses. He arose with what appeared to be a disappointed look only then to proceed in his previous cascading.

Jimmy and John could contain themselves no more and so moved from behind the shed to follow discreetly in the footsteps of the important-looking man. As they followed, they looked at all the things the very important-looking man had touched; they were all golden, just like the queen's crown; gold leaf petals, sepals, anthers, polyanthus, filaments, stems, leaves and sharp golden thorns.

John looked at Jimmy whose mouth was open wide. He said, "Jimmy this is it, this is what I desire, it's everything. We have seen the truth; we are in the presence of the most ultimate thing that can exist anywhere. If we could possess this, we can be anything, we will stupefy all those who try to do us harm. There will be no limit to what we can do! From now on we will not be aimless wanderers because if we have a sizable amount of this enchantment we will be in the presence of greatness. Look how all the Queen's minions bowed and scraped before her, she understood the power of this golden God. Come we will follow the very important-looking man and see what wonders he is getting up to."

They followed; it was easy, as the very important-looking man left a trail of golden artefacts behind in his footsteps. They spied him sitting at a golden table and they got in behind a pillar in the great room they found themselves in.

John said to Jimmy very quietly, "You go in behind that other pillar over there and that way, we'll surely not be seen, and we can watch comfortably what's going on. I'm a bit nervous if we both hide in behind this pillar, we'll be spotted. You can easily slither across the floor, keeping real low down and slide up and in against that other pillar."

Jimmy replied, "Why would I go slithering across the floor, and in against that other pillar when I'm already against this pillar? What's more, you can't go 'in' the pillar because it's made of stone and that's why they call it, 'the pillar,' get it?"

"I was here first, in against, 'the pillar,' get it?" John replied.

"I was here first," said Jimmy.

"If you were here first, why are you standing behind me?" said John.

"You pushed in front of me, don't you remember that

bit?" replied Jimmy.

John said quietly, "It's just that if you go over to that pillar, up and against it, there's much less of a chance of us being seen and we can view the proceedings at our ease. As things stand at the moment, you're up against me and we're twice as broad as if there was only one of us up and against the pillar, so there's twice the chance of us being seen, and what's more, I can't concentrate on what's going on with you poking into me like that!"

Jimmy replied quietly, "I'm not going anywhere, I found this pillar first it's you who's poking into me, if anyone's to move it's you. You go and slitter across the floor, real low and down you'd be a much better slitherer than me, you're always slithering about the place."

John said, "I've never slithered anywhere in my life, you're more of a slitherer than me!"

Jimmy replied, "If you've never slithered about the place never before in your life, why do you all of a sudden think I'd be very good at it? As though you'd know a good slitherer if you saw one, as if you're a world expert at picking out good slitherers, and yet you've no real knowledge of it because you've never even tried it yourself, now can you answer me that one?"

John was just about to answer something real smart when the very important-looking man raised his head and looked over in the direction of the pillar that the two boys were bickering behind, but they were pretty well concealed and what's more, he was too busy with his own affairs, turning everything into gold.

Jimmy and John quietened down a little, John whispered, "Shush! We'll be found out,"

Jimmy replied, "You shush; you're making all the noise and we've not been spotted so shush and we'll watch from here." So, they watched. The very important-looking man seemed content, but his contentment was seeping away.

He had shown kindness to the maid of a very important woman who unbeknownst to him was the bestower of wishes. For his kindness she offered him a wish, any wish that he may want, and as he was enamoured and bedazzled by gold, he wished that everything he touched turned into gold. And so it was, the roses in the garden, the path he trod, the table he sat at, the chair he sat on. All very fine, but now the bread he tried to eat and the tea he tried to drink all turned to gold.

There was nothing he could touch that didn't turn to gold. His daughter, a princess, for he was in reality, a King, appeared in the room and saw the place awash with gold. Jimmy and John were able to shuffle themselves inconspicuously about the pillar and remained unobserved. The princess was startled and wonderous, but she noticed the disconcerted look about her father, the King.

"Where did all the gold come from?" she asked and he told her his story and how he had been granted a wish, and how he had wished for everything he touched to turn to gold and now, he couldn't even drink a cup of tea or eat a piece of bread without it turning to gold and he was solid sick of the sight of the stuff. The princess moved over and approached her father as though to commiserate with him for his troubles; Jimmy was about to call out and warn her not to go near him, but John intervened.

He shushed Jimmy by putting his hand over his mouth just as the princess ran to her father; she embraced him and was immediately turned into a golden statue. Beautiful, the most beautiful, but solid and inanimate. The King stepped back, aghast. What had he done? He loved gold, he wanted to bathe in gold. It was virtually a fetish, but not this! This was an error, a cardinal error, *'please let time go backwards'* he thought. Time doesn't go backwards; it moves on and the King prayed this golden curse he had wished for could be reversed. He set about to beseech the very important lady, the bestower of wishes to redact his wish and return his flawless golden daughter to her former flawed and wonderful self.

He said to the statue, his daughter, "Don't fret, daughter I will go and do some more beseeching, you will be yourself in no time." With that, he ran to find the important woman who bestowed his wishes.

When the coast was clear John said to Jimmy, "What were you going to do, calling out to that girl, you'd have given us away again."

"What do you mean again? I've never given us away, never. Look at that poor man, I knew what was going to happen and now look, he's gone off in such a quandary and left his daughter, a princess, standing here as a big beautiful golden girl statue."

John said, "I love gold. I love it. Don't you love it? I'm not saying I want to marry it. You can't marry it because it's not human, but I do love it. I think we should leave this place and bring some of this gold with us. It would help us on our journey. It would ward off any of our problems and keep us safe. I think that's what we should do, will do. We'll take the easiest, biggest bit of gold that we can carry comfortably. We'll take it and carry it between us and walk right out the door, who's to stop us, we'll have that gold and everything will be alright and I love it. What do you think? I'm going to do it anyway. You're very quiet."

Jimmy said, "I've never seen you like this before. You seem obsessed. I just don't understand."

John said, "What's to understand? It's just instinctive."

Jimmy replied, "What do you mean instinctive?"

John said, "It's something you can do nothing about, something from somewhere, somewhere? Whatever it is, I adore it, and I think we can carry this golden girl statue away with us. Who'll mind and what difference does it make? If you grab hold of her legs and I'll take the upper part of her, of its body, we can go about our way, everything will be fine."

Jimmy said, "Hold on now for a second, don't you think that the king, that very important man is not going to miss his daughter, the princess, when he comes back from his beseeching of the very important lady? I think we're asking for trouble if we take this statue with us. We could take a few roses or even the chair nobody probably would notice them missing."

"Well, a' dare say you have a point," said John, "but I just think the statue of the princess would be a lot easier to carry if you take the legs and I take the top part of the body. If we take roses, which we could do if you want, we'd have to go out into the garden and we might be seen, and if we take the chair it's too obvious, but with the statue, we could pretend it was a person if someone asked us and nobody would know any different especially as it's getting dark and we can throw this old blanket here, over her to cover her."

Jimmy could see where John was coming from but still, he had his doubts. Whilst Jimmy was debating the issue with himself, John had covered the golden statue with the blanket, tilted it forward and was half-dragging it across the floor.

"Come on Jimmy, give me a hand, it'll be a lot easier if you grab the other end and we'll be off and out of here before anyone's the wiser." Jimmy reluctantly found himself lifting the golden legs of the gleaming princess statue. Off they went out the door, out through the garden and out past the gate, and beyond the post box which was for a guard to guard the home of the King and his daughter the princess, who they were now pulling and dragging as best they could. Sure enough, the sun had gone down, and the light was poor, twilight had descended.

"Halt, who goes there?" cried out a voice from behind the guard post box.

Jimmy and John were startled, but John said, "Ignore it, keep going." They carried on but the voice of the guard was insistent.

"Halt, stop right where you are. What is your business and what's that you are carrying?"

John thought for a moment and then said, "Well ahem, er, it's Jimmy and John we are bringing our sister home. She works in the kitchen, and she was taken ill. We are bringing her home for our mother to mind. She'll be ok after a while when we get her home to bed; Mother will take great care of her, and she'll be back in the kitchen again in a day or so. Don't worry yourself you're doing a great job, we're off down the road here, left and straight on all the way."

"Ok if you're happy then off you go. I can give you a hand if you like?" said the guard who preferred to be sitting behind his box reading his book.

"No, no that's quite alright we can manage. She's very delicate and petite," said John, "isn't that right sis?" With that, he gave Jimmy a kick in the shin and whispered, "Say yes."

Jimmy put on a girly voice and said, "Yes bro... But why are you making my other brother do most of the work? It doesn't seem fair to me. Well?"

John had to think, he said, "Well erm, I'm at the front navigating, I've got to make sure we're heading in the right direction. You relax, I can raise the barrier, it's comforting to realise our glorious King and his family are so well protected." Off they went in the right direction, left and straight and the guard went back in behind his guard post box, sat down and resumed his book.

Off they went, Jimmy and John and the golden statue of the princess as far as the eye could see, which wasn't very far, as night was drawing in swiftly and the golden statue was not very petite at all, but quite heavy and Jimmy said, "Why are we lugging this golden lump around with us, we'd be much quicker if we left it here by the side of the road. What good is it to us?"

"What good is it?" asked John. "What good is it? It, she..." (he corrected himself) "...is the most beautiful, wonderful, glorious existence, either above or below, left or right that ever frequented anywhere, ever, and furthermore, she is petite and delicate, so mind her legs etc., as you go. And what's the rush anyway?" It truly was a troublesome and tiresome journey, but John couldn't admit it, and Jimmy was worn out.

The King had returned home, and he too was worn out with all his beseeching of the very important lady. He lay down for a while and dreamed that today, was yesterday, where his rose garden was fragrant, his tea was chamomile and soothing, and his bread was leavened and crusty.

He awoke with a start. His bed was soft and downy, his pillows feathery and fluffy, his blanket warm and woollen. He touched the golden chair and table and they became wooden and wholesome. He went to his garden and touched the gold-leafed roses, they regained their flushes and their fragrances, permeated his nostrils and made him wish what he had wished for most of all, which was to see his daughter the princess, not the brutal golden inanimate being he had left behind, but the beautiful, scolding, darling girl that he adored. Where was she?

He went into his palace where he had last seen his daughter, but she wasn't there. He called his servants and asked them if anyone had seen the golden princess statue; nobody had, and he ordered them to search the palace and the gardens and make enquiries. News returned to the King that there was no sign of the princess and the only thing stirring that night had been the passing of the two brothers carrying their poor sick sister from the palace kitchens, home to their mother. The King had the guard attend his chambers immediately and questioned him about what he had seen and was duly appraised of what had occurred and where the three siblings were going, beyond the gate, left and straight. The guard told the King he had been reassured, and was confident due to the demeanour and mannerliness, that the three people in question were innocent of anything other than what they had said to him, and that even the sister had spoken quite stridently to one of her brothers during the course of the interaction.

The King thought for a while and considered this last comment made by the guard about the sister to be a little unusual considering the state of her health. As no other evidence of the whereabouts of the princess presented itself, he summoned a search party to go after the two brothers and their sister, in the direction that had been indicated by the guard.

Meanwhile, Jimmy and John were lying fast asleep by the side of the road, with the statue of the princess standing beside them. They were nearly unconscious with all their efforts carrying their trophy, which in reality was not worth its weight in gold as they'd only managed to get a little more than a mile from the palace.

Jimmy had said, "Let's put the princess down for a little while and rest, I can't carry on."

John had replied, "Ok but only for a short time." He hadn't needed much persuasion to relieve himself of the cumbersome statue. They laid down their load and fell into deep slumbers.

The search party came across the three figures shortly after leaving the palace. The two boys were apprehended and the golden statue carried back to the palace and the King. When the King saw his daughter, he cried tears of joy. He approached her, embraced her and astonished all those present, as she returned to her former self, a living vital princess.

Whilst the King swooned about his princess, he ushered away Jimmy and John to be put down in the dungeons. They were escorted by two guards, down a dimly lit corridor, down stone steps, in through the door of a single cell, with a single bed and two buckets placed over by the wall. The cell door was slammed shut from the outside and Jimmy and John were alone again in a familiar situation.

"Why did you not stop me from taking that statue," said John. "You surely could see how vulnerable I was to its charms and brilliance."

"Stop you? Stop you? There was no stopping you! I've never seen the likes of it before, you were virtually frothing at the mouth you were in such a state. I had to help you, you could have done yourself an injury and then you'd have been useless. We'd have been well gone away from this place if we weren't lumping that thing around with us. We could have taken a pocket full or two of those rose leaves and been well gone. No, no, you had to have the biggest, heaviest most awkward piece of tat you could see and look where it landed us, back to square one. Stop you? Ha! That's a good one!" said Jimmy.

"Well at least there are two buckets, there's an improvement," said John even though he was still not sure what they were for.

"Luxury, five-star," said Jimmy in a sarcastic tone.

"Well anyway you did help I'm glad to say," said John, "so thanks, my friend. I'm sorry to tell you though that makes you complicit in the removal of the golden statue of the princess from the palace and as such, you could be charged with actual kidnapping not attempted kidnapping, but actual kidnapping of the royal personage as we did leave the palace grounds with her under our volition, and whilst she didn't put up a struggle our actions could be seen as contrary to the greater good of the royal household, principally the very top of the house. Furthermore, we, yes you and me, sought to deceive a person employed under royal patronage and were successful in that aforementioned deception. In summary and conclusion, I put it to you, that you have defiled the royal honour, that very honour that protects all and sundry, health, safety, happiness and contentment around these parts. Do you have anything to say? What did you say your name was again, erm! Oh! Yes, now I vaguely remember, Jimmy that's it?"

"What does it all mean?" said Jimmy.

"We're banjaxed!" replied John. "We couldn't be more up the Swanee, down the banks, out the door, up the walls, Mammy, Mammy where are you?"

Whilst John raved, Jimmy who could take no more of it slid over to the bed and got in, he couldn't understand how he was being drawn into this crime and felt only innocence. He fell sound asleep. John carried on for a good while but eventually slumped to the floor, beside the bed exhausted and fell into a fitful nightmarish sleep.

A cock was crowing outside their cell window and Jimmy and John raised their heads warily in these unfamiliar surroundings. Jimmy's bladder was full, he went over to one of the buckets by the wall and relieved himself as discreetly as possible.

Only when Jimmy had completely emptied himself did John notice his absence from the bed, he turned around to where Jimmy was zipping his trousers and said, "What are you doing?"

Jimmy said, "Oh! Nothing, just looking at the texture of the wall."

"Since when did you care about the texture of walls?" said John.

"I'm just trying to familiarise myself with my surroundings," said Jimmy.

From without the cell door Jimmy and John could hear bustling activity. There was a jangle of keys, and the door swung open. John stood terrified; Jimmy seemed careless.

"It's your lucky day boys; the King has decided to let you go free due to the return of his daughter. You must leave the palace and the Kingdom and never return, do now and take all that belongs to you with you," said a prison guard.

Jimmy and John were bundled out of their cell and out towards the gates. John requested the use of a toilet, and the guard said, "Why didn't you go in the cell?" The guard escorted him to the nearest toilet, which happened to be an en-suite off a bedroom used by one of the palace staff.

They left the palace and walked leftwards and straight. The guard said to them before leaving, "And don't come back, you can thank the princess for you being still able to breathe tomorrow as she put in a good word with her father for leniency. Goodbye and good riddance."

After a while of trudging down the road, John said, "Well there was no need for that!"

"For what?" Jimmy said. "Good riddance. Good riddance to him as well. And did you hear about the princess and her putting a good word in for us? I'd say she really liked me. Maybe we should go back, and I'll seek a meeting with her and see how the ground lies. Well, what do you think?"

But Jimmy was not interested; he thought, if John wanted to go back, he could, but he wouldn't be going with him.

They trudged onward for a good long while and John finally said, "Do you think she really liked me then?"

"Will you pipe up and forget that episode? It's over!" said Jimmy.

"I will yeah. You should have seen the bathroom the guard put me in though. It was luxury, right off the bedroom, right in the bedroom en-suite you know, top of the range, yes very nice. That's where the toilet is in the bedroom, very gauche," said John.

"Oh! Just like the cell then?" said Jimmy. John looked at Jimmy quizzically. They continued their journey, leftward and straight.

"I still think the princess had a hankering after me," said John, "why would she beseech and plead all night long with the King for me?"

"She didn't do any of that, firstly she merely put in a good word, one word with her father, and secondly it wasn't for you, but for you and me, the two of us," replied Jimmy.

"Yea, but anyone reading between the lines would know it was me she really preferred a' dare say," said John.

"Look you have nothing, as in nothing. You've been wandering around the roads aimlessly and pointlessly for quite a while now guided by whatever thoughts scrape their way from wherever, into your head. She is a princess, as in a princess, adored by a King, her father, he who is above the rest of humanity in his Kingdom. We have witnessed it, and we are only allowed to still be breathing on a whim," said Jimmy in conclusion of the matter, but John wasn't finished.

"I know what you're saying and where you are coming

from, but I really feel there's more to all this than nothing. I certainly felt it with the princess from the moment I saw her. My heart, my being skipped a little. It's only natural from that point she would reciprocate. Even when she was a golden statue, there was something between us, I yearned for her, and I believe she felt the same way for me."

"Well, that takes the biscuit, how can a lump of metal have feelings? Maybe you're just lonely and maybe you're just screwing your desires onto anything at hand and maybe there's not a whole lot wrong with that, like a child adoring a teddy or a doll," said Jimmy thoughtfully.

"Well, I'm no child but I do think there is more, for me, for us. Just to be with someone, someone who has an understanding of what I think and feel," said John.

"Well, that's going to be a difficult role to fill and don't look at me," replied Jimmy.

"Just someone who I could feel at one with, someone whom I could relinquish that feeling of self all the time, someone more important than myself, someone to love, adore," John said in conclusion.

Jimmy thought for a while and said, "That's quite a statement, yes quite something."

They went on their way quietly, John dreaming his dream. Jimmy felt something that had always been there, which he hadn't been totally aware of but now was manifesting itself at the forefront of his mind, John had stoked up Jimmy's emotional self and he too began to dream.

Beside their way a sign appeared, it said, "Welcome to Verona."

Chapter 4
Romeo and Juliet

Jimmy and John stepped their way into Verona, a busy city, sights and sounds were seen and heard, and they were astounded. The citizens too were astounded by the two unusually apparelled apparitions before them and amongst them, but by and by they carried on with their business, for life goes on. Stories continue also and the boys had no right to be in a Shakespearean Verona, but there they were, all stories arrive from another hand, for stories are conglomerations of many tales. They took note of everything. The ways of the Veronese people amazed them. They dressed strangely and spoke in riddles it seems.

They overheard a dark-haired, brown-eyed young man (his name turned out to be Romeo) laughing with his friend. They followed them discreetly. He was accosted by two others, there was talk of a ball, a dance, a welcome to all, so long as your surname is not Montague.

"You may'st bring these strange creatures if thou dost desire," said the stranger talking to Romeo and referring to Jimmy and John.

Exit stranger and his accomplice.

"Who may'st you be?" said Romeo addressing Jimmy and John.

"We be'ast Jimmy, (pointing to Jimmy) and John,

(grimacing)."

A slightly confused Romeo said, after a moment, "So anon till yonder sun dost descend, below Earth's cradle ne'er beyond come my friend (addressing his friend), let us depart. This night may'st carry adventures of the heart."

Exit Romeo and his friend (Benvolio).

When they had gone Jimmy said to John, "Did you hear that, did you? What a rigmarole. You'd get on really well with that Romeo fellow."

Exit Jimmy and John.

John was delighted with the way things were going. They had been in Verona for such a short space of time and already they were to attend the grandest of occasions. Furthermore, Jimmy had admitted to him, just now, that he could mix with the Veronese elite, who clearly Romeo was one of, and following on from that, per sé, he had the demeanour required, the skills set so to speak, to mix in the highest of Veronese social circles. Just so. Jimmy was, on the other hand, a little worried that John was losing touch with reality, but what reality?

So anon, the sun has shone, its shine today,

To a ball they must attend,

O'er' this tale shalt' ne'er end, forsooth.

But what about their attire?

"We will stick out like sore thumbs," said Jimmy. "What will we do?" John had been thinking about this.

"We can go as we are, and if we are questioned, we

can say we thought it was fancy dress, and say to the person questioning you — 'And what did you come as?' That should throw them for a few seconds in which time you can move along, and they'll take no more notice because there'll be loads of other things to take notice of."

Jimmy and John duly attended the ball of the Capulets, dressed in the ways of the sanctum where they come from.

"Whom may'st you be?" enquired a portly announcer.

John replied, "We be'ast Jimmy (pointing to Jimmy) and John. We be'ast invited by one said colleague of thine. Please be so grateful as to attend to our outer garments and accommodate them in thy cloisters. We shall strive to purport no further attendance. So long and farewell, and infinite scorn to those bedevilled Montagues."

"Aye, aye", said the announcer, and to all, "Tis' Jimmy and John herein." The boys bowed and held their hands in acknowledgement. The people were startled by their appearances for they dressed in an unfamiliar fashion and held themselves in a most unusual way. John ushered Jimmy aside next to the wall of the ballroom.

"Say nothing Jimmy and just follow what I do, I have the measure of them."

Jimmy said, "Be'ast that be the case, John?"

"Yes, we will observe their moves and before you know it, they will follow our lead. Hush now for a while let's see the sport."

Jimmy and John truly were very good dancers but this dancing before them was a foreign affair. However, just as they had learned the footsteps of their youthful dance, they grasped this new format fluently and rapidly. They danced and danced and danced and all about them were pleased to see such enjoyment. Enjoy it they did. They twirled and swivelled, bowing this way and that and they made such an impression on the Veronese people at the ball, that they were whispered about behind open flat hands, they were virtually the beaus of the ball.

The title of the best beau however fell to Romeo. His belle, the belle of the ball was Juliet. Jimmy and John stood aside and observed and swooned and would have it no other way for they were mesmerised by the two darlings of humanity, who had not yet met, nor were aware of each other's existence but were destined to be, and to be once more. Juliet did dance and did talk with Romeo that fateful evening. Romeo and Juliet. Juliet and Romeo.

Jimmy and John stumbled away from the ball with the rest of the people. The night sky was clear, and the moon shone brightly so the roads were well-lit. They moved slowly and chatted as they went.

"All seemed to go very well," said Jimmy.

"Didn't I tell you they'd be eating out of the palm of my hand in no time," retorted John.

"Surely, be'ast you did," said Jimmy. "You had their

ways and dances off in jig time. I think I could almost bring you anywhere and all would go well; well apart from the time we nearly got eaten by a big growling Papa Bear and the time you landed us in the cells and nearly had us turned into unsightly corpses."

John took no heed of Jimmy's words for his thoughts were on another matter, that of the most beautiful being he had ever encountered, Juliet.

Just then as they were walking John spied Juliet on her balcony. He indicated to Jimmy that they should hide themselves behind some bushes. Juliet surely was a wondrous sight to behold. John nudged Jimmy and placed his right index finger on his lips to indicate for him to be quiet because he could sense Jimmy was a little bit fidgety. Jimmy nudged John and indicated to him to shush. Juliet could hear and see a bit of commotion behind the bushes and called out.

"Is it you Romeo?"

The boys remained silent and still.

Juliet spoke again, "Where are you, Romeo?"

"Over here," called out John, "I'm in behind the bushes."

"Show yourself, you don't sound a bit like Romeo to me," said Juliet.

"I've got a bit of a cold, and my nose is all stuffed up," said John.

Juliet's father who had been behind Juliet in her boudoir unbeknownst to her, called out to the guards,

"Seize him, it is that wayward murderer Romeo." The guards seized both Jimmy and John.

John said, "We're not Romeo."

Juliet's father said, "Then you are worse than he

pretending to be someone who you are not, to such a love-chaste child. To the cells with the deviants. We will deal with them in the morning. You may not be the enemy of our family, but you are the enemy of humanity. How do you plead?"

John took it upon himself to reply, "Not guilty, I only wanted to hold her hand. To hold anyone's hand."

"Well, why didn't you hold your footman's hand?" replied Juliet's father.

"I'm not his footman and there is no way he's holding my hand," said Jimmy.

"You fail to see the disgrace of your activity. I fear there is no redemption for you," said Juliet's father.

"That sounds serious," whispered Jimmy to John.

"There is nothing more grave. Take them away, they will be dealt with at noon of the morrow." Juliet's father left the boudoir and Jimmy and John were led away to the cells.

Jimmy and John found themselves in a single prison cell, with a single bed and a single bucket once more.

Jimmy said to John, "Why on earth did you have to call out to the girl Juliet? Did you not know that you'd give away our position?"

John said, "Well I'm sorry but I just don't know what came over me. I didn't see the harm. How was I to know Juliet's age?"

"Well, you're just not allowed to pretend to be somebody who you are not, especially when it involves someone so young and innocent," said Jimmy. John was quiet for a while. All he ever wanted was to hold her hand. To feel the first touch of their little fingers, turn into a firm charming innocent holding of hands, a mutually joyous hand encounter, and no more. This would be sufficient for him to embrace in his mind's eye forever more. He realised however harmless his intention may have been, he had been wrong. He was truly sorry and said to Jimmy that upon reflection, he was wrong, and he would never let it happen again.

Jimmy muttered to himself and hoped that they could get out of there. John was sobbing pitifully. Jimmy told him to lie on the bed and try to get some sleep. John lay on the bed and sobbed himself to sleep, with his face turned into the single pillow. Jimmy lay down beside him on the ground and slept fitfully.

They were awoken the following day by the sound of the cell door's peephole opening. The prison guard asked them what they would like for their breakfast.

John, who was now quite refreshed said, "Well what have you got?"

The guard replied that they could have whatever they wanted.

"Anything?" said John.

"Sure, anything," said the guard. John called out to Jimmy, who was lying uncomfortably and contorted on the floor.

"Jimmy, did you hear that? We can have anything we

want for breakfast."

"Anything?" said Jimmy.

"Yeah, the guard said we can have whatever we want," said John. They were both ravenously hungry as they hadn't eaten since the porridge so they each reeled off a list of twenty courses of their favourite dishes. Sure enough, all their requests were duly supplied. During their meal, they chatted happily.

"Maybe they've had a change of heart and are sorry for imprisoning us. I mean this is the best meal of my entire life," said John.

"Yeah, I think they've seen the error of their ways. They probably realise you're only a harmless fool with all that blubbering and sobbing you were carrying on with all through the night," replied Jimmy.

John wanted to ask what he meant by that, but he was too busy gnawing at a big greasy pork chop and carried on chomping his breakfast. After an hour of eating, they could eat no more and slumped down into two chairs which had been brought in with the food. They had never been as happy in their entire lives.

John got up to sit on the bucket and Jimmy said, "What do you think you're doin?"

"I'm going to the toilet on this bucket as there's nothing else, and would you mind averting your eyes for a few minutes whilst I'm on the bucket, I'm about to explode," John replied.

Jimmy said, "I want to go as well, I'm going first."

John said, "I thought of it first so it's only fair that I go first."

Jimmy said, "But I thought of it first a long time ago, but I was a bit shy, I knew what the bucket was for all along and what's more, you're always trying to make me go first, so I'm going first."

This argument went back and forth for a few minutes. Fortunately, as it was getting nowhere, the cell door was unlocked and in stepped the guard accompanied by a Franciscan Friar. The Friar told them he was there to hear their confessions. Jimmy told him he had nothing to confess.

John whispered to Jimmy, "What about not telling me about the bucket?" Jimmy nudged John and whispered that he should tell him about the girl Juliet on the balcony. John explained the situation to the Friar, and that he was truly sorry about what had happened the previous evening and he asked the Friar if he could possibly relay his apologies to the girl for his behaviour, and to plead for forgiveness on his behalf.

The Friar said, "Unfortunately the girl Juliet is no more, her love Romeo is gone also in the most tragic of circumstances. It was a feud between the two families of Romeo and Juliet that led to their deaths and their beautiful affair is done for, but their tale of love will live on forever more."

"Oh, Dear! Oh, Dear!" said John "Was it my fault at all?" The Friar allayed his fears on that score but had to relay to them that they were to be hanged from the scaffold to the death, at noon that day.

"What?" they both exclaimed.

"On what grounds? We did nothing wrong!" said John. "Romeo and Juliet's families need somebody to blame and unfortunately for you, you find yourselves in the wrong place at the wrong time. I must go now. I have several other prisoners to attend to." The Friar took his leave with the guard and the cell door was slammed shut.

Jimmy and John looked at each other in despair and tears began to well in John's eyes. The blame game was over, there was no point anymore, all was lost so it seemed.

"Jimmy, you've been my one and only true friend. Through all my messing up, through thick and thin, never mind all the others especially Timmy and Tom who are long gone but who we knew well, you alone have stood by me always by my side," said John.

Jimmy replied, "Well I didn't have much choice in that, considering I was usually locked in a single cell with you."

John was blubbering uncontrollably again and Jimmy held him gently in his arms and placed his face into the front of his right shoulder and gently patted and stroked the back of his head and consoled him. "There, there, John, don't you worry we can get out of this. Don't we always manage somehow or other? Something greater than us seems to be watching over us and looking after us." Deep down Jimmy wasn't so sure, things truly looked bleak.

The key to the cell door released the lock barrel and into the cell once more stepped the Friar. He ushered Jimmy and John to follow him and prepare themselves to meet their makers. Whilst they didn't know what he was talking about, they prayed as hard as they could like they had never done before, to something or someone. They were taken by the Friar down a dark corridor with light at the end, followed by the prison guard. The corridor led into an arena filled with a bad-tempered growling crowd, demonstrably foaming at their mouths. Their object was to take Jimmy and John and rip them apart limb from limb, for they had been told that Jimmy and John were the two ghastly, vicious, demonic and satanic perpetrators, responsible for the deaths of Veronese and humanity's finest, most wondrous beautiful visions and saintly apparitions ever to appear anywhere ever at any time. Not only had the diabolic, fiendish, murdering, scum of the planet, the whole solar system and the universe, been responsible for the deaths of the pure Romeo and fair Juliet but also the destruction of the innocent and yet so tender love of said Romeo and Juliet, which had barely reached its ascendency.

The guards had to hold back this baying crowd for if Jimmy and John were got at here and now, not all would see the spectacle and for that, a platform had been assembled to clearly show the end of Jimmy and John.

They were led up onto the scaffolding.

John whispered to Jimmy, "You go first, you'd be better at it than me."

Jimmy said, "I've never been here before, so I don't see how you can say that!"

John said, "Well what I mean is that you'd exhibit a lot more dignity than me and I could learn from you and I wouldn't be such a jabbering wreck." As they looked at the scaffolding, they noticed two nooses; their destinies were to be completed simultaneously. They were very scared, terrified; their abdominal cavities were whipping their contents of porridge and a one-hour sitting of the best of fayre, like a butter churner. It was at this point that the head of the Montague family, old Montague himself and his former mortal enemy, old Capulet stepped forward linking arms, shaking hands, kissing each other on their cheeks and generally making a display of warm hospitality. Montague took to the platform and began to speak to the fevered crowd.

"Today," he started, "we introduce a new era, an era of great and solemn friendship between our two houses. The loss of our children in such tragic and horrendous circumstances…" On saying these words, he looked over at Jimmy and John, "…has brought a new sense of realisation that his distasteful dispute between our great families serves no purpose but to the detriment of us, and you all. So today, I say with a heavy heart, let us all forgive past discrepancies, let us embrace this new time of peace and reconciliation, let us move on to new chapters and verses in our voluminous tale, let us talk no more of bad will, only goodwill, let us reach for a purity of love like the great love shown to each other by our own flesh and blood now departed, but forever enchanting children. Together we can create a whole new era to progress our lives and the lives of our children, and our children's children." Now it was Capulet's turn to say a few inspiring words and he didn't disappoint.

"My good prestigious friend and ally, I wholeheartedly and unreservedly concur in the strongest of terms with everything and all that you have enunciated so stoically and comprehensively. Furthermore, with this wondrous reconciliation, these peaceable gestures between our two families of sublime people, may I say from the deepest depths of my being..." Jimmy and John were churning away big time, the more the platitudes were dished out the more their eruptions were imminent. "...this friendship nae I say this love, this perfect alliance may it go down in history as a template for all resolutions from henceforth till eternity. Hurrah, hurrah and hurrah." The once pyretic crowds pounded with cacophonic cheering, hugging and kissing and a pouring out of genuine love and care. Old Montague stepped forward once more, gesturing to the crowd to settle for a while.

"Now to cement this new alliance may we usher in this new peace by finally relieving ourselves of our old warring ways with the extinction and execution of these

two murdering despicable miscreants once and for all."
The crowd roared approval. Jimmy and John were led to
their nooses, old Montague himself placed the noose
around John's neck, and old Capulet likewise around
poor Jimmy's neck. The old men retired directly behind
the condemned boys in order to get a real good look as
they fell down writhing through the trap door and the
long drop. Jimmy and John were asked if they had any
final words.

John said, "I'm so, so sorry,"

Old Montague winked and nodded at old Capulet for
the benefit of the crowd.

John continued, "So, so, so, so, so sorry but I can't
hold it in anymore." With that, his bowels erupted its
contents right through his thread-bare prison smock all
over old Montague.

Jimmy said, "Me too." He could hold it in no more
and disgorged everything that was inside of him all over
Old Capulet.

The crowd en masse turned away disgusted, they
couldn't watch and didn't even dare to take a peeking
view of what was happening up on the hanging platform.
Nobody could come within 10 yards of Old Montague
and Capulet; the stench was mesmerising and the two old
behemoths staggered about the platform retching and
vomiting.

With that Jimmy removed his noose, jumped down
from the platform and ran as fast as he could through and

past the backward-looking crowd whose eyes were all closed anyway because they couldn't countenance the reality of what they had just witnessed. John followed in Jimmy's speedy footsteps. They ran right up Verona High Street, turned left at the junction and ran straight on like their lives depended on it, which they did. They ran and ran and ran, right past a sign by the roadside stating, 'You are now leaving Verona, thank you for your visit. Please call again soon.' They jumped into the river Adise to cleanse themselves and their spoiled smocks and continued their journey away from Verona. They bypassed a garbage bin on top of which were their old clothes, so they grabbed them and changed into them very quickly and continued running until they could go no further and fell into a well-concealed burrow. They were utterly exhausted but relieved and slept promptly and soundly.

John woke up to the birds singing after several hours of peaceful rest. He dreamt of happy times, of simplicity, of no cares. His waking hours were nightmarish. Fear prevailed the odd sense of friendship, love, and satisfaction but ultimately fear and death stalked, presaging a violent ignominious end.

He woke Jimmy and told him of his thoughts. "Every waking moment is terrifying. This is no way to live. At home, we would be dead, but at least we would have died with honour heroically, maybe we should think about returning home. We could go quietly, sneak in and see what's going on. Maybe the C.O.S.Y. could be glorious, what are we clinging onto this existence for, it's pitiful, tragic, tortuous. Well, what do you think Jimmy?"

Jimmy wasn't thinking too much, he was all creased up in the burrow, his body ached. It was all very quiet apart from John droning on again. He pulled himself up and out of the hole, and stretched his legs and arms. The weather was fine and he didn't feel any threat. They'd been through a lot over the past day or so, just to relax felt good.

"I'm not sure John," he said, "it's a long way and if we are caught there'll be holy hell to pay."

"But maybe we'll be used as an example. Our experiences could be used to confirm that there really is nothing other than the life we were destined to live from day one. Maybe it is our destiny to follow the path, set out for us, I mean what's so great about our experiences outside of the sanctum? We've barely escaped execution in one form or another on four occasions! It's terrifying, I can't keep up. I couldn't take another near-death experience, nobody wants us, we're out of place. The only distraction I get is when I'm asleep, and that's getting difficult because the moment I'm awake, the terror seeps in again. Jimmy, I want to go home. We'll be really quiet, no one will know, we'll just creep around. We may see a friendly face or two. At least we'd be on familiar ground. Come on Jimmy please, please let's go home."

Jimmy wasn't convinced it was such a good idea, "As of this moment there is no threat, nothing to fear, all these near-death experiences that you're experiencing occur because of some madcap, barmy escapade you think is such a good idea at the time, but which turns out to be just that, foolish in the extreme. If you could just settle for nothing and don't go poking your nose into where it's not wanted, life would be a lot more relaxed, so just try and say nothing for a prolonged stretch and see all those terrors you're living through will go away," said Jimmy. But John wasn't finished, it was not within his nature to stay quiet for any length of a stretch.

He tried another tack. "I think we may have offended our forefathers, the forefathers, by our actions in leaving the sanctum in such a hasty fashion, the way we did. Maybe all the terrors and troubles we've found ourselves in since then are directly related to our behaviour. Maybe like you said there does appear to be somebody or something watching over us, maybe the forefathers are everywhere and can see and hear everything and are controlling our affairs. These forefathers, yours and mine, are our people, our relations, our flesh and blood. They would allow no harm to come to us but likewise, they will not make our passage easy. They want us to return. Remember that we are their direct descendants and as such they have parental and grandparental and so on... love. Yes, Jimmy I said love, they love us, and they know what's best for us. I say to you now Jimmy, right where we are, right in this present moment that it is our duty, and our calling to return home to redeem ourselves before our ancestors. We will be revered even more for seeing the error of our way. Jimmy, I say to you one final time, hear my entreaty, let us journey home to seek out whatever it is that's our destiny, come, come, come Jimmy my dearest friend, nae my brother."

Jimmy was wavering now that John had put it like that, he wasn't sure he knew the meaning of all the words John had uttered, and he was damn sure that John didn't know the meaning of a lot of the words either, but the way it was said, with such earnestness, and passion he felt himself being swayed and he said, "Yes John if you feel so strongly about it and with such a fervour I think, I wish to go home also."

Chapter 5
Home and the Terrible Truth

Jimmy and John are home, home sweet home, the place where the heart is. They had to lay low, keep down and study how the land was lying. How they would be received if their presence was revealed, they couldn't determine.

John said to Jimmy, "Let's get in behind this fence. It would be a good vantage point."

Jimmy replied, "How do you mean get 'in' behind it? You cannot get in it as it is a flat fence."

John said, "Oh! please, not that again, just get behind it."

They hid behind the old hideout, vantage point fence, where they couldn't be seen, but could see what was going on, on the other side of the fence through secret spy holes. Out of nowhere suddenly they spied Tommy and Tim, their old friends, who had left the Sanctum in such a heroic fashion in the C.O.S.Y., never to be seen again. Yet there they were, not much more than an arm's length away, as clear as day. Tommy and Tim walking around. Yes, it was definitely Tommy and Tim.

John said, "Do you see who that is?"

Jimmy replied, "I do."

John said, "I can hardly believe what I'm seeing, but I'd swear that's Tommy and Tim."

Jimmy said, "It's Tommy and Tim alright, but how can that be? They departed for the greater good of all in the Capsule of Spiritual Yearning, and here they are right before our eyes. Yet I don't feel sure, maybe somehow, we are being deceived."

John replied, "Get up and go over to them and see what they say."

Jimmy said, "Why don't you get up and go over? They liked you better than me!"

John said, "You go, you are much more of an approachable person than me, and they'd be more open if they see you coming along. Yes, you'd be much better at it than me."

"How do you mean; I'd be much better at it than you? As though you've been studying our interpersonal relationships and interactions, as though you're some sort of social observer and very astute in this sort of thing. I think as you are so keen to meet Tommy and Tim and you suggested it and I'm not really that bothered, you should get up and talk to them," Jimmy replied.

John, not to be outdone with Jimmy's logic said, "Why don't we both get up and go over and talk to them and see what's going on, surely you must be a bit inquisitive. I mean it really is quite incredible and earth-shattering that Tommy and Tim are here wandering around when we were all led to believe they'd gone off to greater things, never to be seen again! You get up first and I'll be right behind you, yes just one pace behind so it really would be like we were both together getting up."

Jimmy said, "How can we both be together getting up if you are one pace behind?"

John replied, "Well I'll be minding the rear, making sure nothing happens untoward from that direction. We have to be very careful and proceed very intuitively and surreptitiously, covering all possibilities. We are in a super vulnerable position here."

Jimmy replied, "We'll both get up together, and that means at exactly the same time, you proceed in a leftward direction as that's your favourite, and I can't say fairer than that, and I'll go right, how does that sound?"

Before John could answer Jimmy confirming or denouncing his plan, they heard a noise behind them and the old hideout fence. They looked back and there was Tommy and Tim looking at them from behind. They'd heard all the commotion that the boys had been creating and came over to see what was going on, by coming round the back of the fence, and in behind the boys, who were too busy arguing to notice.

"Tommy and Tim, so good to see you both. I'm surprised, amazed to see you. We thought you had gone forever never to be seen again, and yet here you are. Wonderful. Did the C.O.S.Y. not work, did it break down, what happened? Tell us. Tell us!" said John.

Tommy looked at Tim, and Tim looked at Tommy both with blank faces.

"Yes, it's good to see you," said Tommy, "do you

mind waiting here a moment? I just need to ask Tim something."

Tommy and Tim stepped aside, but Jimmy and John shuffled over a little so that they could just about catch what Tommy and Tim were whispering about.

Tommy said, "Who are these two strangers and what are they doing in the Inner Sanctum?"

Tim discreetly ushered Tommy to move further away; he felt they may have been listened to.

Tommy continued, "These must be the two miscreants who blatantly skipped away from their duty and date with destiny. They must be apprehended and placed away securely until such a time as their future can be determined. Pretend nothing is unusual, and that we know them. I'll call security."

Whilst they were whispering and were now out of earshot, Jimmy very quietly said to John, "They're not very friendly, are they? I think they think we are strangers, and did you hear mention of an Inner Sanctum? I don't like the look of this, it's all a bit familiar."

John replied, "Yes, just a slip a' dare say. Don't worry just play along, they're probably just as shocked to see us as we are to see them. Let me do the talking. I'll be able to put them at ease and smooth it all over, I'd be pretty good at this sort of thing."

Jimmy said, "I thought I was the approachable one who they'd feel much more open with. What happened to all that?"

Before John could reply, Tim came over to them.

He said, "It's a lovely day, really lovely as usual."

John replied, "It is Tim, it's really lovely surely."

Tim said, "I'll just go over and see what Tommy's up to."

Tim moved off over towards where Tommy was, covertly calling security from his device.

Jimmy said to John, "What was that all about? What was he on about? 'It's a great day, really lovely as usual', sic."

"I don't know, but I'm just playing along with it, playing the game, per sé. It's all about saying something but really saying nothing. It's highly technical really, and very skilful. Don't say anything that could trap you and catch you out at a later date. Remain neutral at all times and look innocent." John concluded.

With that six automated security personnel arrived and surrounded Jimmy and John.

"Take them away to the holding cell until we decide how to proceed," said Tommy.

It surely was very familiar to Jimmy. Another single cell, another single bed and another single bucket in the corner, which John was sitting on. He had seen it on entering the cell, and decided to expunge himself before there could be any argument from Jimmy, who didn't bother making a fuss as he could see the smug, relieved look on John's face.

"What did we do wrong this time? I thought those two tyrants, Tommy and Tim, were our friends. They behaved as if they didn't know us, and what is all this talk of the Inner Sanctum? It certainly doesn't look like the Sanctum, our home, so where are we?" said Jimmy.

"I don't know," said John. He continued, "Usually when we want something, truly desire it, it happens. We both wanted to go home and yet here we are in a foreign environment."

"I don't understand something though John," said Jimmy, "you really wanted to come home, and I was uncertain at first, until you persuaded me of what a good idea it was. Why didn't you just go if that's what you truly wanted when you knew of my doubts? Why did you feel that you had to persuade me to go also?"

John thought about this for a while and then hesitantly said, "Well I, I, er, I, well I didn't want to leave you on your own, I wasn't sure you'd be able to manage without me there to guide you."

"Thanks for your guidance again by the way, but haven't you noticed where it usually leaves us? Try and guide us out of here because things are looking a bit grim at the moment and I just can't figure out what is going on," said Jimmy.

"Let's look at things logically for a moment," said John.

"That'd be a first," retorted Jimmy.

John ignored Jimmy and went through the facts as he

saw them. "Number one," he said, "number one, we were standing on the scaffold waiting for our execution, when I had the quickness of mind, not for the first time I might add, to utilise the only weapon at our disposal in such extraordinary circumstances, and in so doing relieved our predicament in more ways than one, pertaining a portentous escape in a formidable fashion, ahem!"

Jimmy wanted to know how many steps there were in this trail of John's repertoire of logic. He doubted there would be a conclusion for quite a while.

"Number two," John announced solemnly, "I'll say one thing, we made a hasty retreat to a safe haven and decided in a very astute, and might I add, courageous fashion, that all our roaming and ramblings had led us into more and more precarious and deadly finalities. Thus I, we, decided to return home to the place of the ultimate finality of all finalities and a trip in the C.O.S.Y. and look at what that stands for, Capsule of Spiritual Yearning. It could not have been put better even by, 'the great bard' himself, the person whose diabolic imagination we had such a close encounter with. Furthermore, isn't it a continuance of something alive, something altruistic, a yearning for spirituality, an indefinable desire for something tangible and not nothing? We cannot countenance nothing. So wherever we are, we are within touching distance of that great trip with destiny. The great and the good, our forefathers, the Originals on down through the generations have laid out a plan, a beautiful scheme for each and every one of their children, to follow in their footsteps, to spiritual yearning, to spirituality."

Jimmy had long stopped listening to John's logical sequence which appeared to be running out of steam at number two, and was scrutinising the holding cell for security vulnerabilities, and when he tried the door handle, the door opened.

"John," Jimmy said, "John the door is open, we can get out of here and have a look around, see what's going on." John's train of thought, which had been in logical mode, was broken, to his disgust. He looked over at Jimmy by the open door, he was astounded.

"Close that door at once!" he said, "What are you doing? Can't you see and hear that I'm trying to work this out in a logical fashion, what's going on?"

Jimmy replied, "We don't need logic to solve this, we can go out of here and snoop around and gather all the leads required."

John wasn't satisfied. "In reality, there is nothing to find out. Our destiny is predetermined and that is the end of it."

"How do you explain Tommy and Tim then, and their carry-on? No, John, I'm not happy with any of it and I'm going to take a look. You can come if you wish, or you can logic yourself into a corner over there on the bucket." With that Jimmy made to leave the cell. John reluctantly followed in his steps. In truth, he didn't fancy being left behind.

They began snooping around. Jimmy was in the lead; he kept down and low and motioned for John to follow suit. John didn't like being told what to do and he said, "I should stay a bit more upright so that I can get a good early look at anything that may be coming into view from a higher level."

Jimmy said, "It would be much better if we keep down and low because that's the way I've seen it done, and it makes much more sense for us to be low because then there would be only half a human in view as opposed to the full height of a single human."

John said, "I don't agree. I think if you proceed in the fashion that you are now advocating as being the most favourable, then if a threat does appear from high up, we won't notice it. We have to cover all bases in a situation such as we find ourselves in, we just don't know where exactly our Achilles' heel is per sé, a'dare say."

"As the lead in this excursion, I am the head snooper and therefore I say we keep down and low," said Jimmy.

Before this discussion could go any further voices could be heard from around the corner. Jimmy got down real low and secretly peered around the corner so that whoever was around the corner, wouldn't spot him. It was Tommy and Tim and several other familiar faces.

"What are we going to do with Jimmy and John in the holding cell? In all our existence in the Inner Sanctum, this situation has never arisen, it's uncharted territory."

These words were spoken by a tall, handsome young man. He proceeded,

"From what we've heard of their conversation recordings they will fall for it if we tell them they can still climb aboard the C.O.S.Y., and travel to their ultimate glorious destination. John is definitely bought in and he will persuade Jimmy eventually of the appropriateness of such action. They are good specimens and their bodies will be fully utilised by an original. They can be placed in the refrigerated stock cupboard and kept until required. What else can be done anyway? It would be a shame to dispose of their bodies, any other way. They will become one with their ancestor's brains after transplantation, sharing and caring with their kith and kin." With that final comment this assembly of ghouls, let out a collective unseemly and sarcastic snigger, and a, "hear, hear," and smugly proceeded in righteousness to tell Jimmy and John of the 'good news', that they could speed away under these special circumstances in the C.O.S.Y. after all.

Jimmy and John, who had kept well hidden behind the corner, had heard it all. They were stunned and aghast and it took a while for this terrible truth to register.

Jimmy turned to John and said, "Well what do you make of all that?"

John was ashen grey and gibbering nonsense to himself; he couldn't make an attempt at a reply. At this moment he wished they hadn't gone about this snooping excursion. He wished they were still behind the closed door of the holding cell, like being in a waiting room for a jaunt in that glory mobile the C.O.S.Y.

Jimmy could see John was in a state of shock. He said, "John you heard, now let's get out of here any way we can." He pulled John by his arm and led him away, outward.

Meanwhile, the Originals had discovered the empty holding cell. This cell had been built to imprison any unknown personnel who breached security; the first time it had been used was by Jimmy and John. It had sat vacant despite aeons of time elapsing since its construction. Automatons programmed for security had been developed subsequent to the cell's construction, but because nobody had ever breached security and the cell lay idle, no one had ever keyed into their software to lock the cell door.

An alarm was raised and the automatons set to apprehend Jimmy and John, but Jimmy and John were fairly adept by this stage at making an escape, even in spite of John's tardiness because of his confused state of mind. John followed Jimmy like his life depended on it, which it did.

They proceeded keeping down and low, outward, away from the Inner Sanctum. They came across a secret security door which had one-way access only. They pushed it open and went through. The secret door had never been used and was only built just in case communication was ever needed between the Inner Sanctum and the Sanctum.

Jimmy and John immediately recognised the Sanctum, the old familiar places and beings but they continued down and low and weren't noticed. Now was no time for, 'catch up.' Their desire to return home had brought them to the Inner Sanctum, and into the bosom of their forefathers, and their true beginnings. They moved swiftly and adroitly and reached the point where their journey had started. Jimmy turned right and John followed, right and straight.

Chapter 6
The Garden of Eden,
and the Point of Everything

Part 1

Jimmy and John's concluding big chat, subsequent to recovery from their escape.

Jimmy:- We've had another escape, and who was it this time only our own.

John:- A terrible thing.

Jimmy:-You're back to yourself then.

John:- A' dare say.

Jimmy:- What does it all mean? All our lives we believed. All our lives we have been fools. Yet when we believed we were content and knew no better. Now I know the truth, I feel a torment. I am tormented.

John:- Look Jimmy, you were saying before, how could I have gone home alone, because that's what you thought I wanted. I did want to go home, but not alone. Companionship means everything. Your companionship even.

Jimmy:- Even?

John:- Well, I don't mean that, I mean what's the point if you're alone?

Jimmy:- You're not addressing the current situation

i.e. that we've been had all our lives and on the other side of the secret door they were laughing at us, and the C.O.S.Y., and our heroic exits, and whatever else springs to mind.

John:- A'dare say. I was devastated and shocked there for a while, but I mean we are on the road again.

Jimmy:- It doesn't seem to bother you too much that even your own flesh and blood, self-proclaimed loved ones, would cut you down in your prime and use you for their longevity, forever. There is no end.

John:- Per sé.

Jimmy:- Per sé? How is that per sé?

John: Per sé relates to something which is part of the furniture per sé. It can't change.

Jimmy:- Well furniture can change. A new armchair, or a table, an upgrade or repositioning old bits and pieces.

John:- It's a figure of speech and doesn't bear up to over-analysis.

Jimmy:- So I was right in the first place. You may as well finish off your figure of speech with Percy. He appears from nowhere and makes no sense.

John:- You just don't get it do you?

Jimmy:- There's not much to get.

John:- We could start again. Wouldn't it be great to go back to the beginning, and start it all over, take a different direction?

Jimmy:- Well, we have. We've gone right and straight, my way. So?

John:- I'm thinking of the bigger picture. You know, everything. Not left or right but everything.

Jimmy:- What do we know about everything? Everything! Hoorah! Haha!

John:- We can only speculate as to how it all began before time, yes before time, but there was a time before time when everything was good, a time to hanker after, to be part of, that could be our final destination.

Jimmy:- That's fanciful thinking. How do you suppose we go about arriving at our final destination?

John:- Everything we were led to believe was a lie. We must clear our minds of all our previous notions. Eighteen years of nonsense notions, think of nothing.

Jimmy:- Ok that shouldn't be too difficult.

John:- That's funny a' dare say, but do we want the old way?

Jimmy:- How you change.

John:- We have to move on. It was our duty to die at Eighteen years of age.

Jimmy:- It's hard to move on. Our Father's, Father's, Father's Father's and so on, used his son's and grandson's bodies as his own. It's unbearable.

John:- Bear it we must. As bad as it may seem, we must move on.

Jimmy:- How woeful? Woe, woe, woe.

John:- Enough woe, we are gifted you and me Jimmy, gifted.

Jimmy:- Hmmm?

John:- We know the truth. We have confronted the perpetrators of that terrible truth. We should be dead, yet we aren't, we are still here chatting. What's more, we have been and seen. Let's go again, back to a time before the originals, before their annihilation of the Earth's crust, before their demonic attitude to one another that led to their scurrying away down the, 'slippery slope', into a hole in the ground.

Jimmy:- Does such a place exist John?

John:- I hope, I wish, I desire it to be so, but Jimmy you must do also, I can't leave you here now alone. You know you can't get by without me.

[Jimmy tries to interrupt but John ploughs on.]

We, you and me, Jimmy and John, the two great gifted, nae gifts of and to the Earth, Solar system, Universe and any other highly unlikely but definitely likely planetary pageantry existing out there, we, I repeat you and me shall venture forth once more to, see, hear, smell and touch a most wondrous spectacle. We will feel in our hearts the glorious truth.

Jimmy:- You certainly have a way with words. I'm nearly convinced, but…

John:- No buts Jimmy. Let's suppose we stay as we are, here wherever here is, what then? I can't imagine what that would mean. We were destined right from the start, it's out of our hands; everything that's happened has brought us here, it's not a fork in the road, it's straight, straight on forward.

Jimmy:- You are right John, I do wish and desire, with every sinew in my body, with every red corpuscle and white cell, with all that is me, the thing that you were just talking about.

Part 2

Jimmy and John entered a garden. It was teeming with all the living things, each being more wonderful than the last. It was a garden of pleasure, fruitful and well-watered. This garden was a place of everlasting delight, bliss and happiness. The most beautiful being in the garden was a woman. She spotted the boys and gestured for them to approach her, which they duly did, and introduced themselves to her and she to them. Her name was Eve.

Eve was perfect in every way. She explained that the garden was the Garden of Eden and everything they needed was there and they could stay and live here. They had never; seen, heard, smelt or touched anything more fulfilling. This was the Earth's crust which they had been taught in 'The Sanctum' was uninhabitable yet here it was flourishing. Eve explained that following the nuclear and environmental holocaust people left behind by the 'Originals' had survived meagrely in a hostile environment, but survive they did.

As time passed by, slowly, very slowly the Earth's regenerative powers, unhindered from the blemishes, bruises and insults caused by the 'Originals', recovered its magnificence, for it truly is hard to kill a good thing, especially when the bad thing has departed.

Eve told Jimmy and John to go and take a look around, she would prepare a welcome meal. Eve was quite taken by the unusually attired young men, strangers, yet friendly and open. Jimmy and John wandered away to explore as directed, they had fallen head over heels for Eve.

The boys wandered a while but not too far, they were mesmerised by the beauty and goodness of Eve.

John said, "Eve is the one, the one and only."

Jimmy replied, "You say that about every girl you meet."

"Ah! But Eve is the embodiment of a woman, she's easy on the eye, kind and welcoming. She's; Mother, daughter, sister, cousin, auntie," said John.

"All very close relations by the way," interjected Jimmy.

"Don't mind that," continued John unabashed, "she's comfortable in her own skin and not ashamed of her own body and what's more she's obviously good in the kitchen, for at this moment she's preparing a welcome meal for us, yes, she ticks all the boxes."

Jimmy replied, "And don't I get a look in?"

John said, "Don't worry Jimmy I'm sure she'll have a friend or know somebody who'll do you."

They heard a rustling sound nearby, it was Eve with a basket collecting fruit and nuts, berries, herbs and other foodstuffs from the garden. They got in behind a broad baobab tree, that was adequately wide enough to fit the two of them without any disputes and watched, because they didn't want to disturb her whilst she was working.

She came upon a mature apple tree laden with ripe red apples. She appeared to hesitate before the tree for a moment and was about to move on, when a serpent snake slithered down the tree. It advanced in an amiable fashion towards Eve. John was about to call out to Eve to beware, but Jimmy ushered him to say nothing as there didn't appear to be any malintent in the situation and calling out may startle the snake which then may strike. It appeared to be conversing with Eve, but the conversation was out of earshot of the boys.

"Say sssssister," it hissed, "seems like you're having guests for dinner."

"Two boys passing by lost and in need of nourishment," she replied.

"The best nourishment in the garden is the fruit of this tree," said the serpent.

"But I don't think I should take it, I have been warned not to, it is forbidden," said Eve.

"Don't mind that, that's just for pussies," it said.

"Well, if it's ok with you, I think I'll move along," insisted Eve.

"Sister don't be sissy. Listen to me, those two boys
behind the baobab tree think they are hiding from you

and me, we both know they are there. As well as nourishment they need shaping up a little. A bite of one of my succulent apples will embellish their mental agility, (not difficult), beyond, over and above. You see Eve I'm only looking out for all of you," the serpent concluded.

"They're not your apples," said Eve, "you've tried this one before and look where that led us, not to a garden of delights but to a garden of frights and fights."

With that, she grabbed the serpent by its neck and thrust it down. She stood firmly on its head, clutched hold of its tail, raised the snake, and hit it against the ground several times. Whilst still holding its tail she approached the edge of the garden, swung the serpent about her head, around and around like an athlete swinging an Olympic hammer, and caste it down the 'slippery slope', through the Sanctum and the secret door, which had been left open by the boys, and on into the Inner Sanctum. She roared after it with a banshee-like wail, "Go to hell, and shut that secret door behind you! Don't show your hissy face around here anymore!"

The boy's eyes nearly popped out with astonishment; she was certainly some woman to be reckoned with.

Jimmy whispered to John, "Are you sure you'll be able to manage her?"

Before John could attempt an answer, Eve said, "You may come on out now Jimmy and John, it's gone down and away to be with its friends. Gone forever more, I'm not so sure, but for now, we will prepare a feast to celebrate your arrival and the departure of that slippery serpent."

They feasted on a sumptuous fayre, for Eve indeed was very good in the kitchen. Jimmy sat to Eve's right and John to her left. She laughed and smiled and thoroughly enjoyed their company, especially Jimmy who she found quite charming. He was chatty and a good listener, funny, easy-going, kind and open-minded, whereas John was quite hard work, a little shy, but sweet.

The boys wanted to know how things in the garden remained so tranquil. Eve explained that there were certain guidelines that they should follow if they were to remain here in contentment:

1. Share your porridge, there is enough for everyone, but never ever steal Papa Bear's porridge.

2. Don't believe everything the 'mirror, mirror on the wall', tells you it can change from one moment to the next.

3. Enjoy what you have, great possessions can weigh you down. Having few wants is happiness.

4. Love in all its guises should be nurtured and encouraged today, tomorrow and forever more.

5. If you come across a big red push button and you don't know what it is for, don't press it.

Eve departed from the boys briefly, for she had to go to the little girl's room.

Jimmy said to John, "Come on we'll clear up here. I'll

do the wash-up, and you can dry."

John said, "I'll wash you can dry, I'd much prefer washing, it's one of my specialities, I used to get a right good shine on the plates, everyone used to talk about them."

Jimmy replied, "Do you really believe that, that everyone used to talk about your shiny plates, I never heard anyone mention them."

John continued, "Oh yes! I was really rather well known for it, for them shiny plates. They shone brilliantly and squeaked when you rubbed them. They were an absolute pleasure to eat off, the metal of the knives and forks used to chime against the glazed surface of the porcelain plate, it added to the whole mystique of a fine dining experience."

Eve arrived back without a single plate being cleaned. She was stunning and shimmered through the room. She asked Jimmy if he would accompany her through the garden, for a late evening stroll, there were a few things she wanted to share with him. She asked John if he would mind washing up, he could leave the dishes and pots to drain. She told him her younger sister would come by later as she was in the habit of coming along every day.

Eve and Jimmy sauntered off leaving poor John all on his own. They were gone all night; John was fretful, not because he was worried but because he was lonesome. He knew that Jimmy was smitten by Eve, his own heart panged but the die had been cast, and he had to accept the inevitable. Eve and Jimmy, Jimmy and Eve. Oh! How lonely John felt he had yearned for companionship and here he was washing dishes and pots and pans on his own.

As the night passed by, John paced a little, sat down a lot, and tried to sleep but could only toss and turn restlessly. This was to be his lot he thought. In the gloom John could barely perceive the sun was beginning to rise, a new day was starting. What appeared to be a female outline was moving towards him, he fixed his gaze, yes it was a female figure. She came out of the night into this early morning and right over to John.

"What's your name?" she asked, "My name is Dawn."

John was in awe of Dawn for she was the most beautiful and precious sight and person he had ever seen. They chatted amicably about this and that and John prepared tea and cakes leftover from the feast of the night before. They hit it off from the start.

Dawn said to John, "Come and walk with me, I can show you all the pleasures in the garden, there are many and we can share them together."

John was a little nervous about leaving this place and the pots and pans and dishes but what the heck. Dawn held out her hand. The little finger of John's left hand gently touched and caressed the little finger of Dawn's right hand, and he could just about discern the whorls of her fingerprint. Their hands slowly embraced each other intimately and John allowed Dawn to lead him on her path. It was all he had ever wanted.

Jimmy and John are now leading separate lives, their adventures together are over. Jimmy is with Eve, and John with Dawn. They still meet at times for social occasions or just bump into each other. The last time Jimmy met John, he asked him how he was doing.

John said, "I'm doing very well, a' dare say."

Jimmy said, "You know those things you keep saying, a'dare say, and sic, and per sé can you put them together in a single sentence without any other words, and for it to make sense?" John thought for a while and confessed that he couldn't.

Jimmy replied, "Percy's sick, a' dare say."

John said, "That's very clever, but how did it all happen to us, you and me Jimmy?"

Jimmy said, "What you think of and dream of, you become."

They went home that evening, John with Dawn turned left, and Jimmy with Eve turned right.

About The Author

I was brought up in Rainhill near Liverpool. My parents were Irish and I was reared in an Irish tradition. I was well-schooled principally by Irish nuns and Christian Brothers who devoted their lives to God. After school, I attended The Royal Dental Hospital in London qualifying as a dentist in 1983. In 1988 I followed my parents and sister home to Ireland, to the Medieval capital of Ireland, Kilkenny, where I met and married my beautiful wife.

In 2016 I finished work and after 33 years of running around chasing my tail and raising my three children, there is nothing I like more than relaxing, including gardening, golf, playing cards, reading and writing.

A short story I wrote was published at, XR Creative.org in February 2021, titled, "I was a Plastic Bag." Two further short stories, "The Darling of the Dog and Duck", and "Communication Meltdown" were long-listed in a writing competition in the West of Ireland. My poem, "The Bits in Between, (by the Bride's Father)", was published in an American journal in 2023. "Journey To The Surface Of The Earth" is my latest novel published with Blossom Spring Publishing.

www.blossomspringpublishing.com

www.ingramcontent.com/pod-product-compliance
Lightning Source LLC
Chambersburg PA
CBHW031944170626
46807CB00015B/3103